For Lane Smith and Molly Leach
pals, rain or shine

Printed in the United States of America
Reinforced binding

First Edition, October 2008
20 19 18 17 16 15 14 13 12 11
FAC-034274-16140

Library of Congress Cataloging-in-Publication Data on file.
ISBN 978-1-4231-1347-8

Visit www.hyperionbooksforchildren.com and www.pigeonpresents.com

Are You Ready to Play Outside?

By Mo Willems

An ELEPHANT & PIGGIE Book
Hyperion Books for Children/*New York*
AN IMPRINT OF DISNEY BOOK GROUP

2

Gerald!

4

5

7

We are going
to jump!

NOTHING CAN STOP US!

It is starting to rain.

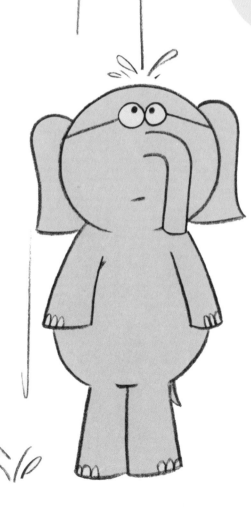

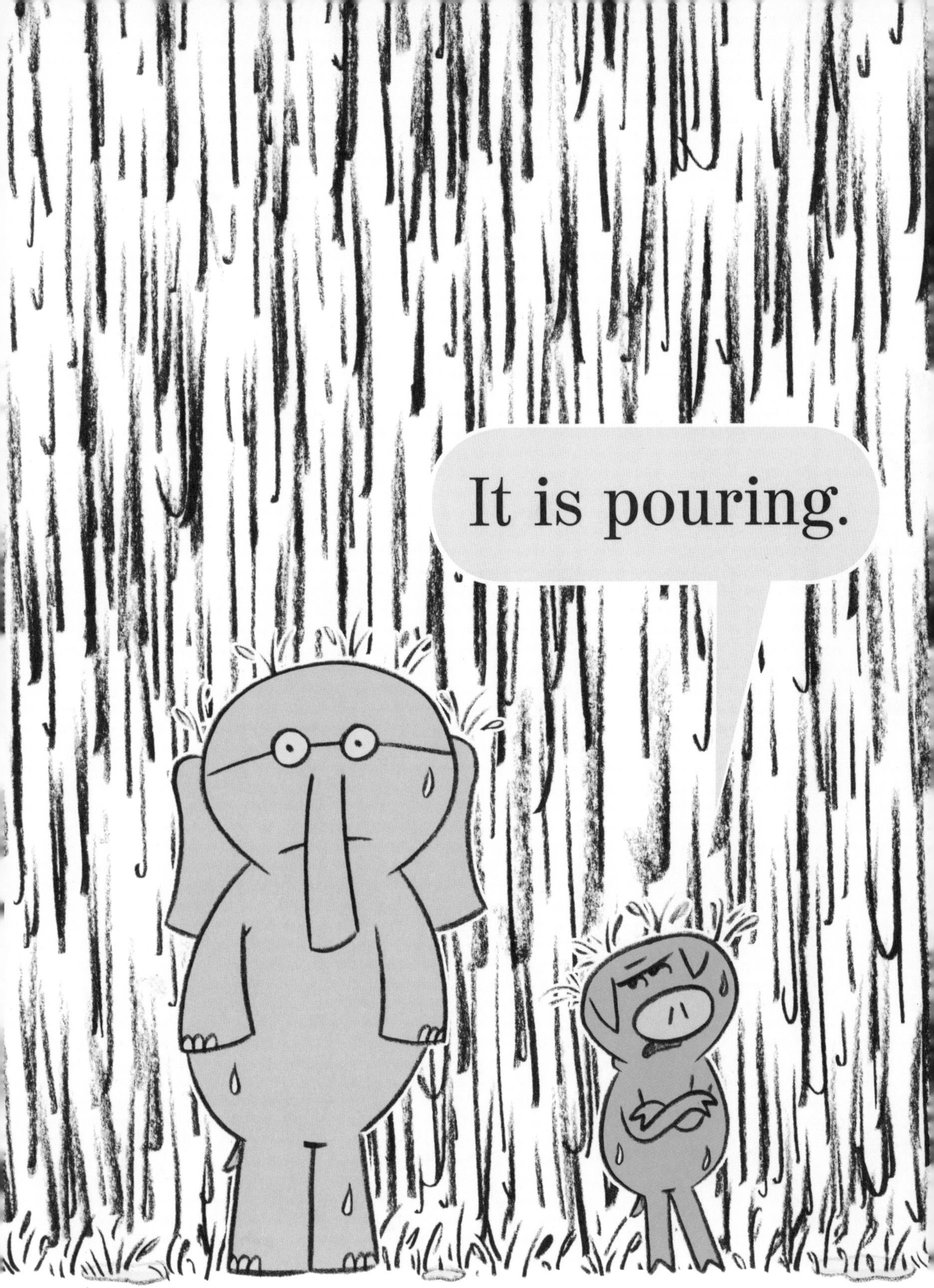
It is pouring.

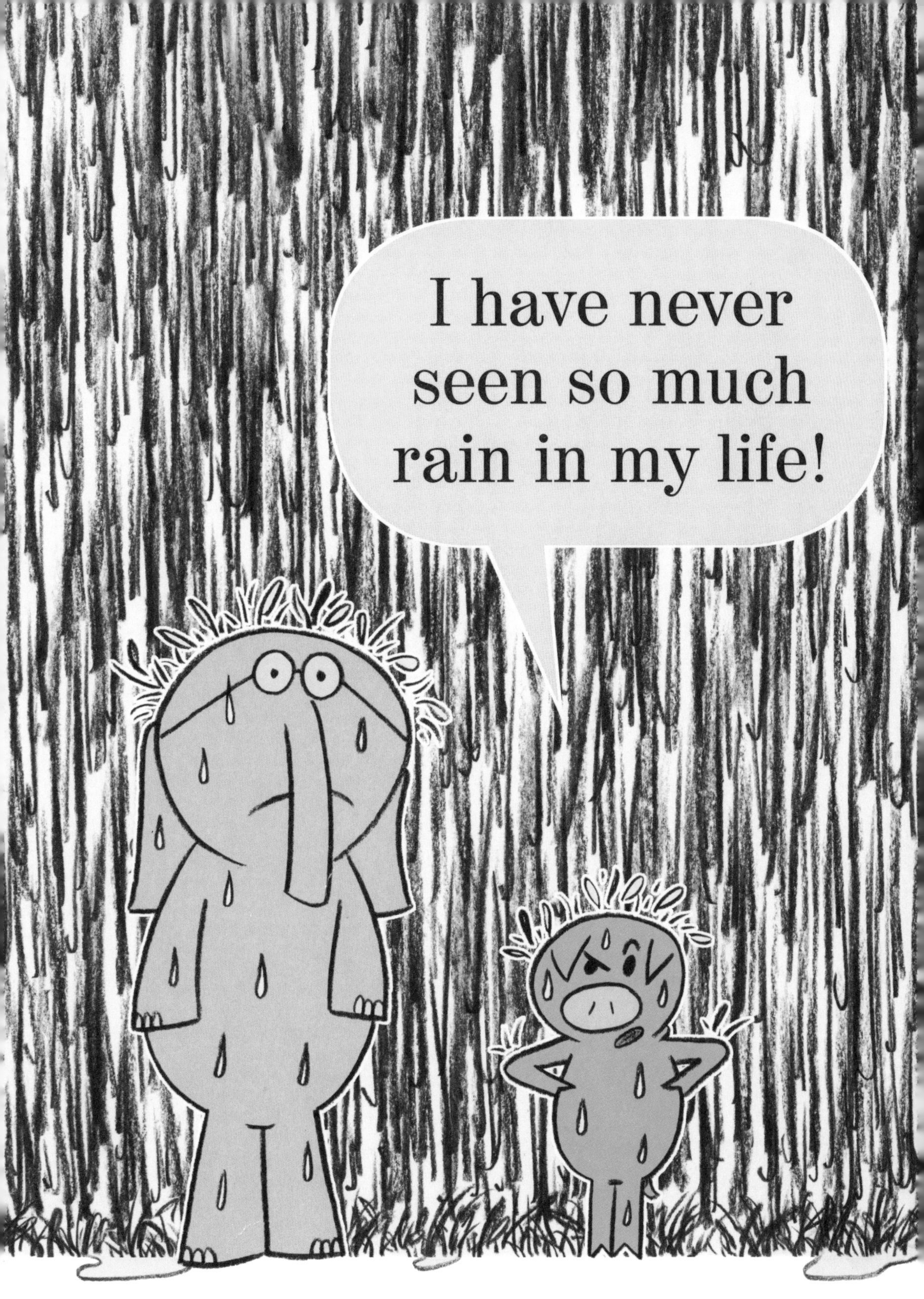
I have never seen so much rain in my life!

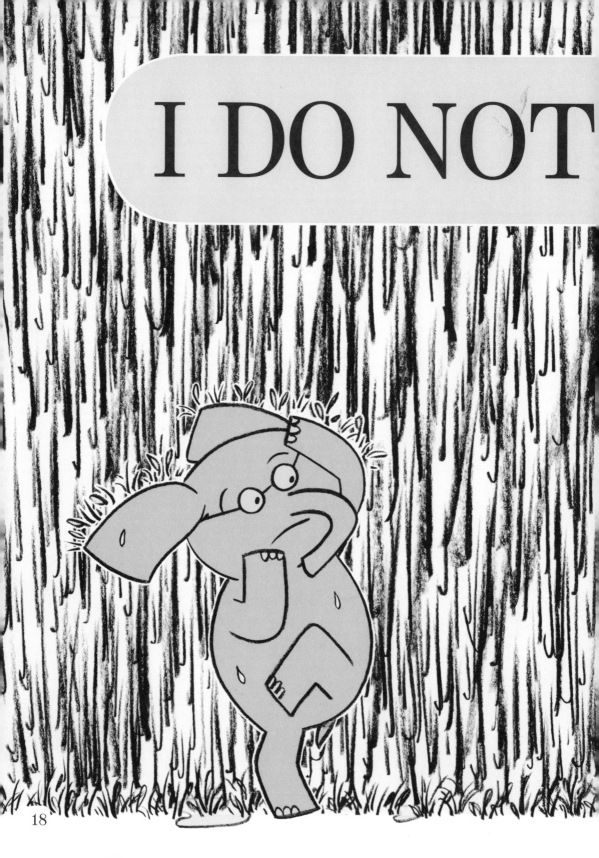

I DO NOT

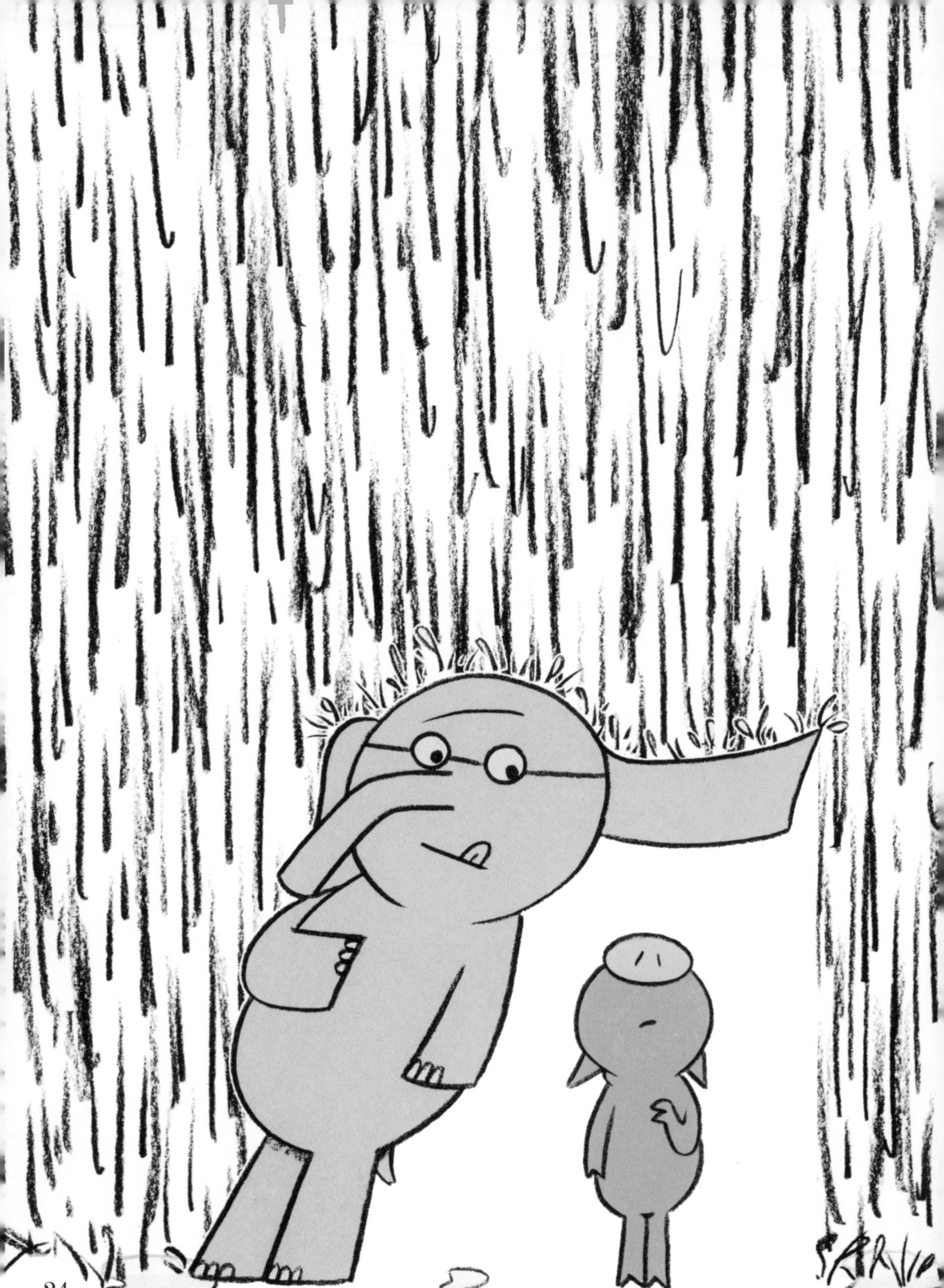

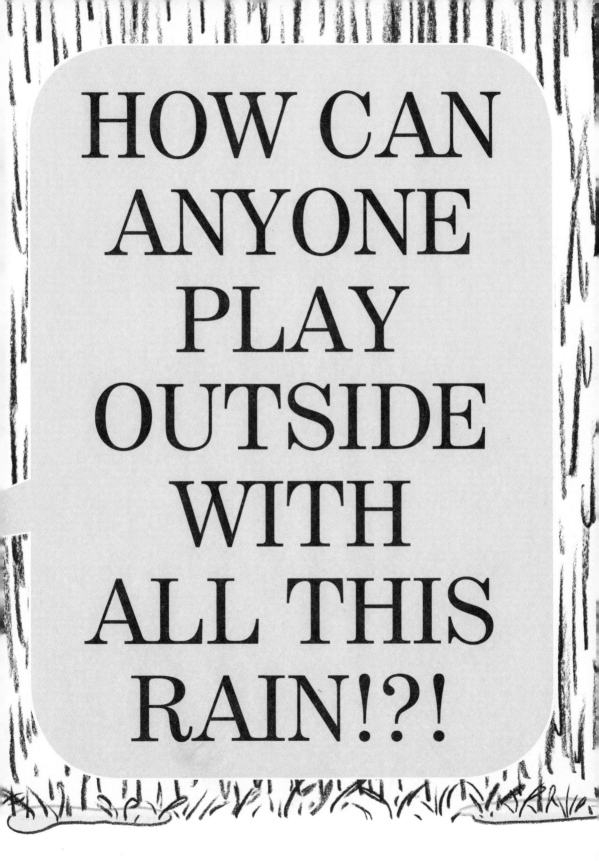

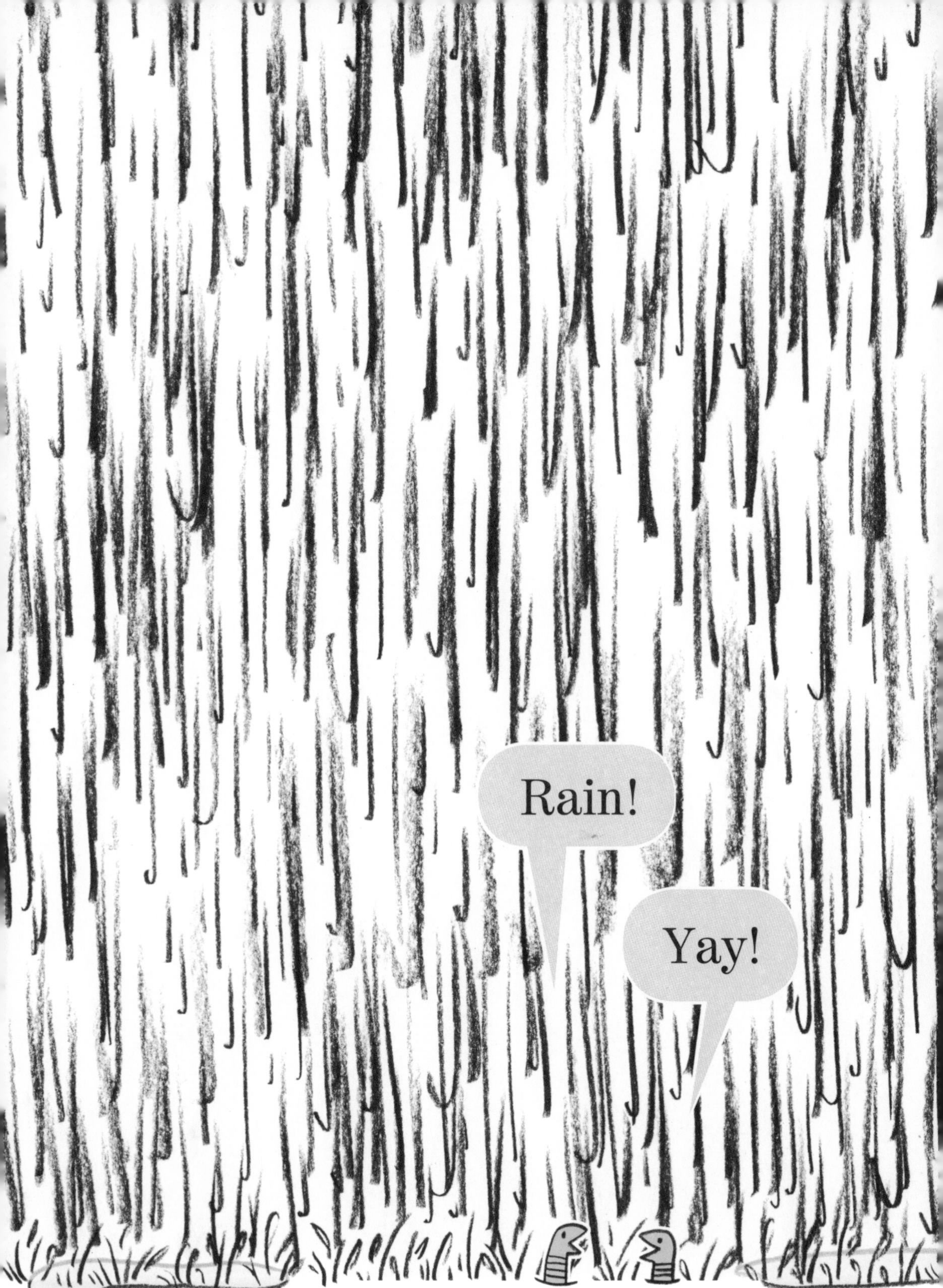
Rain!
Yay!

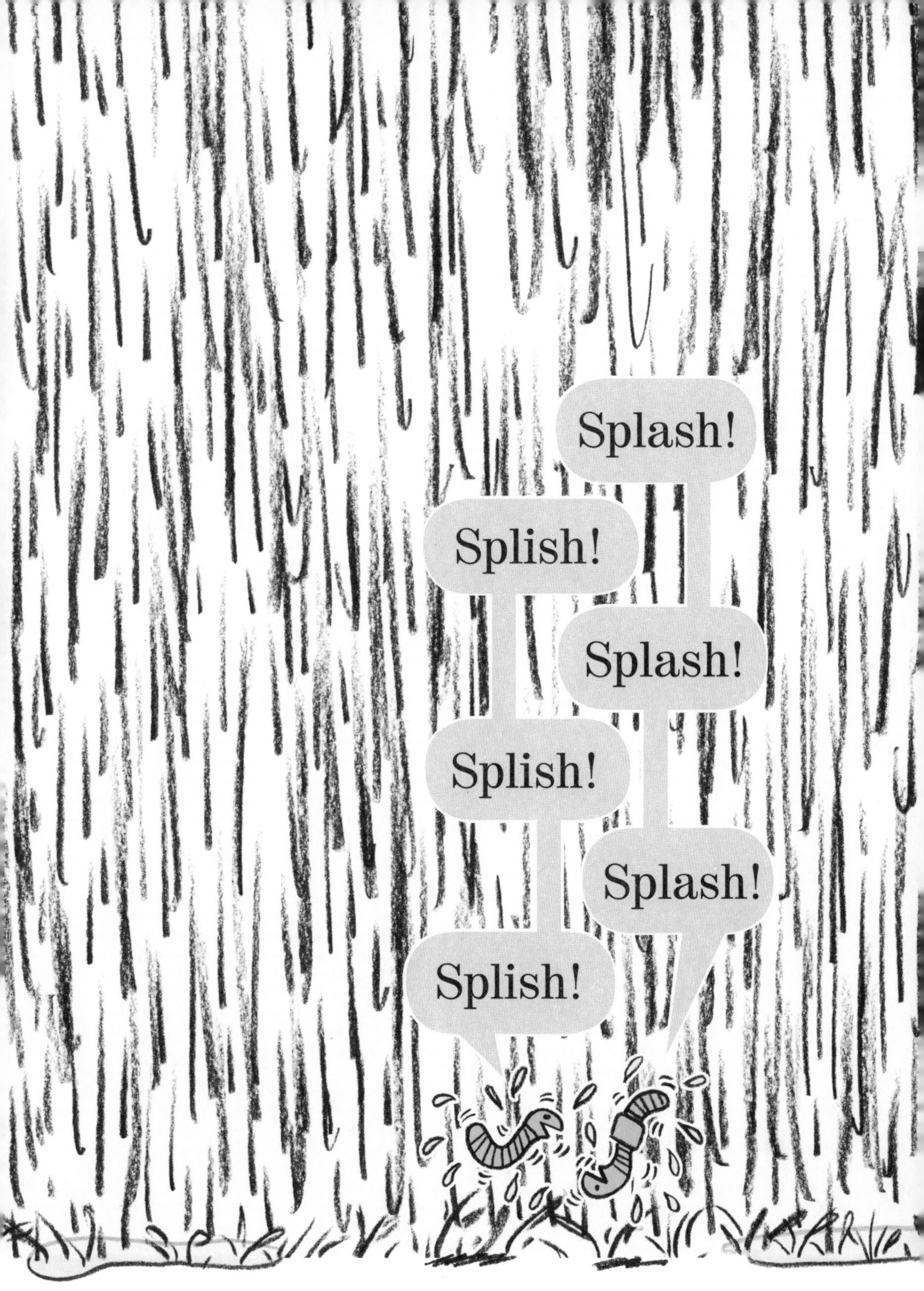
Splash!
Splish!
Splash!
Splish!
Splash!
Splish!

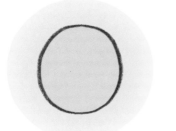

Rats.

and now the
rain has
stopped!

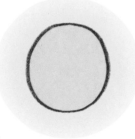

I am not
a happy
pig.

52

Do not worry, Piggie.
I have a plan.

Have you read all of Elephant and Piggie's funny adventures?